'This is speculation, but we believe at age one your son may be around age four, and this will continue throughout his life,' Dr Lin explained to the Powells. 'So by age five he could appear to be an ordinary, fully grown twenty-year-old man.'

Brian and Karen looked at each other in disbelief. Then they walked quietly down the hallway towards the maternity ward, where their son lay silently in his crib. He was a beautiful, shining baby, and his parents couldn't help but smile with pride.

'We'll call him Jack,' Karen said softly.

Brian nodded his head. 'I like Jack,' he said, and turned to the baby. 'Do you know, you'll be the first boy to shave before you start kindergarten?'

Jack

A novel by *Beth Nadler*

Based on the motion picture from
Hollywood Pictures

Executive Producer *Doug Claybourne*

Based on the screenplay written by

James Demonaco and *Gary Nadeau*

Produced by

Richardo Mestres   *Francis Ford Cappola*   *Fred Fuchs*

Directed by
Francis Ford Coppola

PUFFIN BOOKS

For Doug and Jake
– B. N.

PUFFIN BOOKS

Published by the Penguin Group
Penguin Books Ltd, 27 Wrights Lane, London w8 5TZ, England
Penguin Books USA Inc., 375 Hudson Street, New York,
New York 10014, USA
Penguin Books Australia Ltd, Ringwood, Victoria, Australia
Penguin Books Canada Ltd, 10 Alcorn Avenue, Toronto, Ontario,
Canada M4V 3B2
Penguin Books (NZ) Ltd, 182–190 Wairau Road, Auckland 10,
New Zealand

Penguin Books Ltd, Registered Offices: Harmondsworth, Middlesex,
England

First published in the USA by Hyperion Paperbacks for Children 1996
Published in Great Britain in Puffin Books 1996
1 3 5 7 9 10 8 6 4 2

Puffin Film and TV Tie-in edition first published 1996

Text copyright © Hyperion Paperbacks for Children, 1996
Story, art and photographs copyright © Hollywood
Pictures Company, 1996
All rights reserved

Typeset in Palatino by
Rowland Phototypesetting Ltd,
Bury St Edmunds, Suffolk
Made and printed in England by Clays Ltd, St Ives plc

Contents

Prologue

WHEN JACK POWELL was born he looked like your average baby. His smooth, round cheeks had a touch of pink to them. He had a broad, welcoming smile and his eyes were sparkling blue. But Jack wasn't your average baby at all – not by a long shot. And the circumstances surrounding his birth were far from ordinary.

On Hallowe'en Eve, Karen Powell was rushed to St Vincent's Hospital. She and her husband Brian had been dancing at a fancy-dress party. Brian was dressed as the Tin Man and Karen was dressed as the Wicked Witch. They were showing off their fancy footwork on a conga line, when, all of a sudden, Karen doubled over in pain. She was two and a half months pregnant, and immediately feared something was wrong with the pregnancy. Karen was rushed to St Vincent's Hospital, where she lay on a stretcher, anxiously wondering what was going on.

A stark, white hospital sheet covered Karen. The sheet was draped over her round belly, which made her look as though she were much further along in her pregnancy than only two and a half months. There had been no time for Karen to change out of her Wicked Witch costume, and at the bottom of the sheet you could see her red and white striped stockinged legs sticking out. Brian sat next to his wife and held her hand tightly while Dr Benfante examined her.

The doctor conducted several tests on Karen. It seemed impossible, but all the test results confirmed the unbelievable. At only two and a half months pregnant, Karen was carrying a full-term, nine-month-old baby boy!

Karen couldn't believe what the doctor had told her, but there wasn't time to think about what was going on. The baby was coming – fast! Karen broke out in a sweat. She squirmed in pain.

'I need you to help me,' Dr Benfante told Karen.

'*Aaagh*, it's too soon!' she cried out. Karen's screams echoed through the hospital corridors.

A few minutes later, she delivered a seemingly healthy baby boy.

Tears of happiness ran down the cheeks of the baby's proud parents. Brian was still in his Tin Man costume, and his tears left long streaks in his silver face paint.

'Don't you rust up on me now,' Karen joked.

Brian smiled back at his wife. Then Karen closed her eyes for a bit and dreamed about her son.

'Like you, we've been puzzled by your son's premature birth,' Dr Benfante told Karen and Brian the following day. He then introduced them to Dr Lin, a specialist in infant disorders.

'There's nothing debilitating about your son's condition. He is totally healthy and normal in appearance. Alert and happy . . .' Dr Lin began. 'But his cells are developing at what seems to be four times the normal rate. He may be two and a half months old, but physically, he's nine months and was ready to leave your womb.'

'But he's healthy. I still don't understand,' Karen replied.

'Is he going to age like this the rest of his life?' asked Brian.

'This is speculation, but we believe at age one your son may be around age four, and this will continue throughout his life,' Dr Lin explained to the Powells. 'So by age five he could appear to be an ordinary, fully grown twenty-year-old man.'

Brian and Karen looked at each other in disbelief. Then they walked quietly down the hallway towards the maternity ward, where their son lay silently in his crib. He was a beautiful, shining baby, and his parents couldn't help but smile with pride.

'We'll call him Jack,' Karen said softly.

Brian nodded his head. 'I like Jack,' he said, and turned to the baby. 'Do you know, you'll be the first boy to shave before you start kindergarten?'

1

Ten-year-old Monster?

JACK POWELL WAS almost ten years old. Although he had a curious, young look in his bright blue eyes, his face and body were that of a forty-year-old man. Mr Woodruff was over at the house. He was Jack's full-time tutor. Jack didn't go to a normal school. He and Mr Woodruff spent most weekdays working together on his studies. Lately, though, Jack had lots of other thoughts on his mind that had nothing much to do with schoolwork! Mr Woodruff was growing impatient while waiting for Jack to get back to his desk and continue working, but Jack kept staring out of his window. Outside he saw a bunch of kids from the neighbourhood playing on his family's front lawn. He wondered what they were saying to one another.

Louis Durante was perched in a tree below Jack's bedroom window. He pointed up towards the window, but he didn't see Jack standing there.

'That's where he lives,' he told the other kids.

'You're lying,' said John John.

'He's not a monster. There's no such thing,' exclaimed George as he passed a pair of binoculars back to Louis.

'I'm telling you, he's our age but he looks forty – all hairy and everything. He's like a freak or something,' Louis went on to say.

'Well, why haven't we ever seen him then? If he's our age, why ain't he in school?' asked John John.

'He's dangerous and huge enough to hurt other kids. That's why they keep him locked up. A teacher comes to his house every day,' answered Louis, climbing down from the tree. 'He's like a monstrosity. That's why they hide him.'

'No wonder they keep him out of school. He'd probably wig out and crush us,' said George anxiously.

All of a sudden the boys heard a noise. They looked up at Jack's bedroom window and noticed a figure peering down at them from behind the curtain. Then slowly the window opened and out of it dropped a big, slimy rubber eyeball! The boys made a mad dash towards the street and away from Jack's house. But Louis stood right by that slimy eyeball and stared at it. He picked up the eyeball and examined it for a moment, then walked away with it. Jack watched the kids run off and let out a big sigh.

'That's enough, Jack. Let's get back to work,' Mr Woodruff said as he watched his student moping by the window.

After another sigh, Jack walked back towards his desk. Not concentrating on what he was doing, he tripped on some toys, strewn about the floor. Jack loved his toys. He usually had a blast playing with his action figures, but today he couldn't muster the energy. He stood up and plopped down in a chair beside his desk.

'OK, where were we?' Mr Woodruff asked. But Jack couldn't focus on his schoolwork. Every time he looked down at his textbook, his mind wondered off and his eyes kept turning to his bedroom window.

2
Birthday Boy

O N JACK'S TENTH birthday, the sun's rays
shone brightly and created all sorts of interesting patterns across the grass in the Powells'
back garden. Jack's mum had decorated the
garden with streamers and balloons in all the
colours of the rainbow. The birthday boy stood
out in the garden holding a large stick and then
swung at an enormous piñata hanging from an
old tree branch. Jack's dad and grandfather, who
Jack called Poppy, laughed along with Jack as he
kept missing his target.

Inside the house, Karen was putting the finish-
ing touches on a deliciously gooey-looking birthday cake. Mr Woodruff arrived to join in the
celebrations and watched as Karen added ten
candles to the cake.

'I just want to let you know that I've noticed a change in his behaviour,' Mr Woodruff began. 'He's acting differently. Quieter. As if he has something on his mind.'

'He's just fine, Mr Woodruff. Look at him. He's having a ball. We got the biggest, most vulgar piñata on the face of the earth. We got him a bike and this lethal squirt gun. He's going to be torturing us all day . . . He'll be in hog heaven!' said Karen with a big smile on her face.

Mr Woodruff sighed. He wasn't convinced that his favourite student was 'just fine'. Suddenly, Mr Woodruff was caught off guard. Karen put a big glob of chocolate icing on the end of his nose. She laughed while licking off the bit of icing that was left on her finger. Mr Woodruff then dipped his finger into the glob of gooey icing that was on his nose and smiled approvingly back at Karen.

Later that day, Karen carried the chocolate birthday cake out to the back garden. Ten candles burned on the cake as she placed it on the table in front of Jack. His eyes seemed to glow with the candles as he looked over his cake.

'Make a wish, Jackie,' called his grandfather. 'You're as young as you feel – not as old as you look!'

9

'Make it a good one!' Mr Woodruff added.

Jack closed his eyes, thought really hard, and with one big blow extinguished all the candles. Then, from out of the garage, Brian appeared rolling a shiny red bike with orange reflectors on the wheels and a blue and black geometric design on the handlebars. This was the bike that Jack had dreamed about owning for months. He ran over to his new present and handled it excitedly. Then he gave his parents a big hug – a little too big!

'Ouch!' Karen said, surprised at her son's strength.

Brian turned to his son. 'Watch Mommy's back,' he said. Then they all looked at one another and chuckled.

'I'm going to get you, Jackie!' Karen exclaimed. She ran down the hallway with a flashlight in her hand. 'Marco,' she called out.

'Polo!' answered Jack, panting. He giggled and made a quick dash under his bed. For a moment he thought the coast was clear, but then he saw two feet standing right beside his bed. He was doomed! A bright light shone in his face as Karen bent down and pointed the flashlight at her target.

'Gotcha!' she yelled.

It was a game they often played. Jack and Karen continued to run through the house laughing, until finally they were worn out. They lay on the floor next to each other, breathing heavily.

Karen turned towards her son. 'Are you OK, honey?' she asked. 'If something's wrong you can tell me. Mr Woodruff mentioned something . . .'

'Mom, am I a giant?' Jack asked, catching his mother totally off guard.

Karen didn't know what to say. She looked at her son with compassion.

'No, of course not. Where did you hear that?' she asked.

'Is that why I don't go to school?' Jack continued.

This wasn't the first time that Jack and Karen had had this conversation. Jack had brought the topic up several times before, and each time Karen had found herself at a loss for words. This time was no different.

'Look, we'll talk about this,' sighed Karen.

'When?' Jack asked, practically begging for some answers. But he knew that, once again, the conversation was going nowhere and he should drop the subject.

'Not right now. It's . . .' Karen started to say.

Jack chimed in, '. . . time for bed. Brush your teeth. Put the toilet seat back down.'

Jack gave his mum a kiss and wished her good night. He got washed, put on his most worn-in pair of pyjamas, and crawled into bed, way under the covers. He shut his eyes tightly, and in time drifted off to sleep.

The following morning brought more sunshine and the opportunity for Jack to play outside with some of his new birthday presents. Poppy played along with Jack and watched him as he launched missiles from his new helicopter. Karen stood by the large kitchen window inside the house looking out at her father and her son. She wondered what the future was going to bring for her family, especially for Jack, and made a mental note to remind her son to shave his face today. Her thoughts were interrupted by a knock on the door.

It was Mr Woodruff coming to have a talk with Karen and Brian. Karen expected his visit. She grabbed a mug from the cupboard and poured him a freshly brewed cup of coffee.

'It's a wonderful thing what you've set up

here,' Mr Woodruff said as he took the mug from Karen. He took a sip of the hot coffee. 'I'm not trying to take that away from you,' he continued.

'I know you're not. But to say that he should start going to public school is ... crazy,' Karen responded in an agitated tone of voice.

'Just because he's different doesn't mean he has to be an outcast. We can speak to the school, and they can prepare the students.' Mr Woodruff tried to convince the Powells what he thought would be best for Jack.

Brian sat next to his wife and didn't say much. He was a quiet man and usually thought about things long and hard before giving his opinion.

'But Brian and I have been through this before.' Karen reached for her husband's hand. 'We've seen how people react. I don't want Jackie to have to face that.'

'You know, he has a child's eyes. You ever watch his eyes when he sees other kids? His world moves faster than ours. Don't let it pass him by,' said Mr Woodruff as he picked up his jacket and left the Powells' house.

That night after Jack climbed into bed his parents came into his room to tuck him in. Karen gave him a kiss on the cheek, and Brian gave him a kiss on top of his head. They turned off the light in his bedroom and left the door open a crack, just the way Jack liked it. Later on, Karen and Brian lay in their own bed, talking about their son's future.

'Mr Woodruff doesn't know what he's talking about,' Karen began to say as she went to rest her head on Brian's chest. 'I blame him for filling Jack's head with ideas about going to school.'

'Imagine that – a teacher wanting a kid to go to school. Where do they get such ideas?' Brian smiled as he stroked Karen's hair.

But Karen was terrified. 'You know how children are. They make fun of the fat kid with glasses. What do you think they're going to do to the six-foot-tall hairy kid?'

As soon as Karen finished speaking, there was a knock on the door.

'Mom, Dad.' It was Jack. He opened the door and stood in the doorway dressed in the same kind of pyjamas that his dad was wearing, off-white with little blue birds.

'What's wrong, Jackie? Are you OK?' Karen asked in a concerned voice.

'I'm OK. Just can't sleep. Had a scary dream
. . . Can I sleep in here?' he asked.

Brian moved across to the side of the bed to
make room for his son. 'Of course, buddy,' he
said.

Jack jumped into bed with his parents and got
himself situated comfortably under the warm
covers between his parents. He immediately felt
better. The mattress sunk a bit in the middle of
the bed where Jack was lying. He snuggled
between his parents and closed his eyes. Not too
long after, Jack was snoring away.

'You're sure he's ready for this?' whispered
Karen to Brian.

'Jack will be fine,' Brian said assuringly. 'It's
the rest of the world I'm worried about!'

3
First Day of School

A FEW WEEKS had passed since Mr Woodruff had talked with Karen and Brian about Jack going to school. It was now a blustery autumn morning and Jack's first day of school. There was more chaos in the Powell household than they had seen for months.

'Come on, Jack. You'll be late. Hurry!' Brian called out.

He tripped on one of Jack's trainers on the way down the stairs. He threw the trainer upstairs on to the landing and stopped to adjust his tie. Brian caught a glimpse of his son standing in front of the bathroom mirror, shaving. He went into the bathroom and slid the razor over a bit of stubble on Jack's face. Jack smiled, washed his face off, and applied a bit of toilet paper to a tiny cut. He then ran a comb through his hair, and smiled at himself in the mirror. Jack took a deep breath and left the bathroom with Brian.

In the kitchen, Karen was preparing Jack's lunch. She piled sandwiches into his lunch box. She put in a sausage sandwich, another sausage sandwich, a cheese sandwich, crisps, two apples, four pieces of celery, a container of juice, and five biscuits. Karen could barely close the box! Like the rest of the family, she was more than a bit nervous about Jack's first day at school.

'He'll be OK.' Brian tried to reassure his wife. 'You ready to rock?' he asked Jack.

'Ready, Dad!' Jack said as he grabbed his lunch box, a notebook, and a jacket. He burst out of the front door, ready to face his new world.

The three of them approached Jack's new school together. Jack stood on the lawn of the Nathaniel Hawthorne Elementary School, gazing up at it with nervous excitement. Karen noticed the bit of toilet paper stuck to her son's cheek and removed it for him.

Inside the school, Miss Marquez was preparing her fifth-grade pupils for the arrival of their new classmate.

'As I said yesterday,' Miss Marquez began, 'he may look quite different from all of you, but actually he's just your age ... I want you to treat him with respect and care just like you treat one another, and I hope you'll all be friends with him very soon.'

'It's the giant. He's coming now!' whispered a boy in one of the middle rows. It was Louis Durante, the boy who had climbed the tree on Jack's front lawn.

Jack walked through the corridors of his new school. Beside him walked Mr McGee, the principal of the school, and his parents. Mr McGee was a short man and had to tilt his head back to look at Jack.

'So, Jack, I've heard a lot about you, son.' Mr McGee tried to make polite conversation. 'As principal, I want to welcome you to our school. What do you think of it so far?' He looked up at Jack through his small, grey, glassy eyes and waited for a response.

Jack stared down at his principal and excitedly answered, 'It's huge – it's cool!'

'Yes it is.' Mr McGee smiled. 'Want to see your classroom?'

Jack looked eager, as the four of them came to the end of the corridor and turned left towards Miss Marquez's class. On the way, Karen noticed quite a few stares from teachers and pupils alike peering through their classroom windows. She glared back at the stares and patted her son on the back. Jack didn't seem to notice, though – he was too busy staring at all the pupils' work that hung on the walls.

'Here we are. Ready, Jack?' Mr McGee turned to Jack. They were in front of his new classroom.

'Jack, are you OK? You're sweating. Are you sick?' Karen pulled a handkerchief out of her bag and wiped her son's forehead.

'I'm fine, Mom. I'm fine,' said Jack. But the truth was he was sweating profusely, and his hands were trembling. He made both hands into fists, trying to hide the fact that they were shaking, and then he took a deep breath.

Mr McGee stopped at the door of the classroom. He gestured to Karen and Brian to let them know he had the situation under control and that it was time for them to leave. Brian took Karen's hand and started leading her down the corridor. But Karen walked back over to Jack and gave him a big kiss on the cheek and a reassuring smile.

'Mom! Gross!' Jack exclaimed as he rubbed his cheek with his arm.

'Jack, if anybody is mean to you, just tell your teacher, and someone will call me, and . . . I'll kill them!' said Karen. Then Brian started to tug her down the corridor. 'And don't trade away your lunch,' she called. 'And don't eat anything the other kids give you.'

'Karen!' Brian sighed as he wiped a tear off her face and gave her a kiss. He put his arm around her, and they turned the corner at the end of the corridor.

Jack watched them walk away, and then he turned and looked at Mr McGee and took another big breath. Mr McGee opened the door to Miss Marquez's classroom, but Jack stood out in the hall.

'Come on, Jack. Don't be shy,' said Miss Marquez as she held a hand out to him.

Jack apprehensively entered the room. He looked down at his feet while smiling shyly. He then noticed his principal leaving the room, and Jack took another deep breath.

The pupils were in awe. They couldn't believe what they were seeing.

'Jeez, he looks like my dad,' said George with his mouth hanging open.

'Except hairier,' added John John.

But none of the students laughed. They were much too much in shock to laugh. They just stared at Jack, who stood alone in front of the class.

Miss Marquez walked over to Jack to comfort him. 'Welcome to our class,' she said. 'I'm glad you're here.'

This made Jack's face light up a bit. He already knew that he liked his teacher. She seemed kind, and she was cute too!

'Students, this is Jack.'

A few kids in the class muttered, 'Hi, Jack.'

Jack couldn't believe what he was going through. This was one of the most embarrassing moments of his entire life. Everyone was staring at him. All he noticed when looking out at the kids in the room were eyes! Eyes, eyes, and more eyes staring right at him! Jack looked down at his untied shoelaces, started fidgeting with his hands, and then brushed a lock of hair off his forehead. He spotted a little dust ball in the corner of the room. For that moment, he wished he were that ball of dust or, at the very least, the size of the dust ball. But no, he was big, the biggest thing in the room. Except maybe for the blackboard, but he wasn't sure that counted.

'All right, class. Now I know some of you are a little curious about Jack, so why don't we take some time right now and ask him some of the questions you've got on your minds. Is that all right with you, Jack?' asked Miss Marquez.

'OK. I don't mind,' he answered.

George whispered something to Louis. The other kids looked away from Miss Marquez and shifted in their seats uncomfortably.

'Anybody? Well, I know I've got questions. Jack – when's your birthday?' asked Miss Marquez.

'September twelfth,' answered Jack.

'Well, we've got a lot of September birthdays here. Jennifer behind you is September sixth, and John John, you're what?'

'September eleventh,' muttered John John.

'God! You're almost twins!' Edward teased.

John John glared at Edward. 'Shut up.'

'Let me see . . . are there any foods you just hate?' Miss Marquez asked.

Jack didn't have to think about that one at all. He blurted out, 'Broccoli! Yuck!'

'Anybody else here hate broccoli?' A whole

bunch of kids raised their hands. 'Hmmm . . . maybe you've all got more in common than you think.' Miss Marquez smiled.

A boy in the second row, wearing thick glasses, decided to be brave and ask a question.

'What kind of stuff do you do?' he asked.

'All kinds of stuff,' answered Jack. 'I once got two crayons stuck in my nostrils and almost suffocated.'

That seemed to break some of the tension because all at once, everyone seemed to have a question.

'When you get in trouble, do they, like, spank you?' one girl asked. The kids laughed.

'Can you drive a car?' asked another pupil.

'I wish!' exclaimed Jack.

'When is your bedtime?' someone else asked.

'Nine o'clock . . . I'm working on nine-thirty.'

'How did you get that way?' questioned a little girl in a bright orange dress.

'Well, my mom's pushy. I guess I'm pushy too.' Jack sort of smiled.

'Yeah, pushing forty,' Louis snorted. Everyone started cracking up.

'That's enough!' Miss Marquez said sternly. 'Jack, why don't you take a seat and we can all

get started. Everyone take out your giant book –
I mean your geography book.'

Jack walked over to his seat. He looked at the
chair and thought that it was perfect for a normal
ten-year-old – not a ten-year-old of Jack's size.
He tried to squeeze himself into the seat. No luck.
He tried harder. He wanted to be discreet, but
no such luck. Once again, all eyes were on him.
He wiggled and wriggled and tried so hard to
squirm his way into that tiny chair – but no luck!
Jack stood up and with him came the chair. The
kids were laughing at him. Then Jack lost his
balance and crashed on to the floor – chair, table,
and all! Thankfully, the impact bumped the chair
off his bottom. He became unstuck from the chair
during the fall. Jack looked around him and
smiled nervously at his classmates. Then Miss
Marquez brought him a *big* chair.

4
Playground Blues

Jack's first day of school was almost as hard on his mother as it was on him. Karen spent the day pottering around the house, trying to occupy her time with something other than worrisome thoughts of her son. She assembled a scrapbook for Jack, gathering photos of the family and drawings that Jack had made over the years. After she had finished the scrapbook, Karen decided to bake Jack's favourite cupcakes, the kind that have different-coloured candy pieces in them. Once the cupcakes were done, Karen sat down to have lunch.

Only half the day had gone by, but it felt like for ever. Lunch just didn't feel right. On most days, Karen ate lunch with Jack and Mr Woodruff. Karen noticed Jack's black plastic spider on the kitchen counter. She grabbed it and pretended to feed it a piece of lettuce from her salad.

What am I doing? Karen thought to herself. Then she rolled her eyes and tried to finish her lunch.

Karen's day was progressing pretty slowly, but not as slowly as Jack's. In the school playground, Jack watched the other kids play. He looked around and saw a crowd of girls jumping a rope. In one corner of the playground, kids were playing cards. In another corner, groups of children were standing about, laughing and talking. As Jack took everything in, he noticed that everyone was staring in his direction.

They were looking at him, so he told himself not to look back. Jack stared down at his big feet and the ground. But he couldn't help looking around. There were so many new things to see – things which he had never been exposed to before.

Jack noticed a group of boys from his class. They were the same kids who had been on his front lawn that day.

'Oh, man, he's looking at us,' John John said, trying not to stare back at Jack.

'He probably recognizes us from the street.

26

He's probably planning on kicking our butts,' Edward added nervously.

The only one of the boys who didn't seem to be afraid of Jack was Louis. Louis was staring at Jack, when all of a sudden a basketball hit Louis right smack in the middle of his chest. The ball belonged to Victor and Eric, two bullies from another class.

'Hey, why don't you watch where my ball is going?' asked Victor, who grabbed the ball and stood looking down at Louis.

'That's real funny,' answered Louis. 'Maybe if you knew how to play the game . . .'

'What was that?' Victor yelled. Then he tried to torment Louis by bouncing the ball in front of him and then a few times on his head.

'You know what the problem is, Victor? You have the Zackly Disease.'

Victor looked at his friend Eric, hoping he would know what Louis was talking about. 'What's that?' he asked Louis.

'It means your mouth smells ZACKLY like your BUTT!' Louis held his stomach, he was laughing so hard. The rest of the gang broke out in laughter too.

'That's so funny I forgot to laugh,' Eric said.

He had his hands on his hips and he looked as though he wanted to hammer Louis into the ground.

'Hey, that's new,' Louis laughed. 'You guys ought to save up and buy another brain so you can quit sharing. Losers say "what".'

'What?' asked Victor.

'Loser!' screamed Louis.

'Think you're so tough, why don't you come out on the court and get your butt whipped again?' Victor said as he began to walk back to the basketball court.

Louis followed him and then turned to convince John John to come with him. 'Let's just do this, all right?' Louis practically had to drag John John by his sleeve on to the court.

'Why does he always have to drag me along?' John John asked. 'You know they're gonna cream us.'

Jack had watched the whole scene and followed the boys over to the basketball court. This was the first time he had seen a real school bully in action. Jack took a seat beside the kerb, engrossed in what was happening on the court, when someone came along and poked him in the side with a long stick.

28

'Ow! Stop!' Jack yelled as he pushed the stick away. Then he looked up to see who was at the other end of it. It was a young girl named Phoebe and her friend Jane.

'Are you a freak?' Phoebe asked innocently.

'No,' Jack answered. He didn't seem too surprised by the question.

'Jane says you're a freak.'

'Who's Jane?' asked Jack.

'I'm Jane, and you're a freak.'

'Am not!' said Jack. Once again, Phoebe began poking Jack with the stick. 'Stop it, or I'll tell.'

'How old are you?' Phoebe asked as she put the stick down on the ground.

'Ten,' Jack replied, wishing he were somewhere else.

'You don't look ten,' Phoebe said as she studied Jack. 'I think you're a freak.'

'I *am* ten.' Jack didn't know what it would take to convince the girls that he was telling them the truth.

'That's weird,' said Jane. 'I think either you're not ten, or you're a freak.'

'He's ten. A whole two years older than us. See!' Phoebe said, smiling. She thought she had worked something out.

'Oh, sure, like that explains it!' replied Jane sarcastically. She wasn't satisfied with any of the answers she was getting.

Jane and Phoebe walked away, leaving Jack with his head hung low. His feelings were hurt. Jack fixated on his feet once again. At this point, he knew where every little speck of dirt lay on his trainers, since he spent so much time looking at them! Jack had begun to retie his shoelaces for about the millionth time that day when he saw a basketball roll towards him and stop by his feet.

Louis was calling to Jack from the basketball court. 'Hey, how 'bout a little help?'

Jack looked over at the court and saw all the boys staring at him. Is he talking to me? he thought. Jack was nervous. He didn't know quite how to respond.

'Throw the ball over,' called Louis. His arms were outstretched, waiting to catch the ball.

'Wait, I'm not touching that thing. It's been contaminated now that *he's* touched it!' yelled Victor.

'Yeah, I ain't touching it!' Eric added. He and Victor began laughing, while poor Jack just stood there holding the ball, so frightened he was barely able to move.

Louis and his gang of friends weren't laughing, though. This time they really noticed Jack's pain. Jack wiped off his sweaty forehead with his shirt and was chewing on his upper lip when the school bell sounded. It was the end of breaktime. All the kids ran over to form lines by the school entrance and wait for their teachers. Louis turned and looked over at Jack, then joined the rest of the kids. Jack just stood in place, still frozen.

5
Like Riding a Bike

J ACK'S FIRST DAY of school was finally over.
He came home dragging his lunch box up the
concrete steps to the back door of his house.
Karen opened the door and smiled excitedly at
her son. Jack walked through the kitchen without
even grabbing one of the freshly baked cupcakes
that sat on the counter.

'Jack, I made sloppy joes for dinner and guess
what I made for dessert – chocolate pudding!'
Karen said cheerfully. She turned to her son and
noticed that what she said hadn't even put a smile
on his face.

'I'm not really hungry,' Jack said mopingly.

'Jack, my chocolate pudding! Your favourite,'
Karen tried again. But her efforts didn't work.

'No thanks,' he said. Jack was so depressed he

didn't want to be cheered up. He went upstairs to his room and changed out of his school clothes. He put his grungiest tracksuit on and ran back downstairs and outside. He got his bike out of the garage, hopped on it, and rode around his front garden.

When Jack's dad came home, Karen met him at the door.

'Brian, this is serious,' she said.

'What happened?' asked Brian.

'What do you think happened? Children whispering, pointing. He's not used to that,' Karen said as she paced around the kitchen.

Brian went outside to have a talk with his son. He sat down on the steps to the front porch. The sun was setting, and all that was left to see of it was a small glowing orange ball way off in the distance. It was cool outside, and the leaves on the trees swayed back and forth in time with the wind.

Brian called to his son, 'Hey, your mom made sloppy joes.'

Jack rode his bicycle over to where his dad sat.

'She hates sloppy joes,' Jack commented as he lifted his foot off the pedal and put it on the ground.

'That's true. In fact, all adults hate sloppy joes. But sometimes we make them to cheer up kids who've had a bad day. You want to tell me about it?' Brian asked Jack.

'No.' Jack looked down at the ground and then started to ride away.

'You know what I was just thinking about? The first time you learned to ride a bike. Remember that? You were so determined to ride. Kept wiping out. Nearly took out a couple of the neighbours.' Brian smiled as he stood up and leaned against the railing.

Thinking about that time made Jack smile.

'It took a couple of days until you finally got it, and now you're like a pro . . . It's kind of like school, isn't it?' Brian asked.

Jack nodded as he thought about his father's words. Sometimes his dad made a whole lot of sense.

'Anyway,' added Brian as he began to make his way up the steps to the front door. 'I just wanted to see how you were doing. If you need anything, give me a holler.'

'Dad,' Jack called. 'Could we put up a basketball hoop?'

Brian smiled back at his son and nodded.

*   *   *

That night, Jack, Brian, and Karen had the biggest sloppy joes for dinner, followed by a gargantuan portion of chocolate pudding for Jack.

After dinner, Brian made a makeshift basketball hoop out of wire and some netting he found in the garage. He attached the hoop to an old oak tree in the back garden and put up some spotlights. Then Brian got out the basketball.

'It's all in the wrist, Jackie, like this. We used to play one-on-one in the school playground every day. Just watch.'

Jack watched his father score. Then he mimicked everything his father did and tried to put a make-believe ball through the hoop.

Karen watched her son and husband from the kitchen window. She decided to go out and join them. Karen grabbed the ball from Brian and dribbled it. She went to make a shot, and missed.

'Mom . . .' Jack complained.

'Oh. Uh-huh. No chicks allowed. I get it,' Karen said as she bounced the ball back over to Jack.

'This is one-on-one, Mom . . .'

'Yeah,' Brian added.

'Nothing's changed,' she muttered as she walked back inside.

'Remember,' Brian said as he stood in position holding the ball, 'it's all in the wrist.' Brian threw the ball towards the basketball hoop and totally missed the shot.

6
The Second Day

WHEN JACK ARRIVED at school the following day, he was a bit less anxious. At lunchtime, he brought his lunch box out into the playground where the rest of the kids were. He wandered around for a while looking for a spot to have his lunch and noticed that although there was still a group of kids staring at him, there was a whole lot fewer than the day before. Just then, Phoebe and Jane started walking towards him.

'Not going to poke me, are you?' Jack asked, not entirely joking.

'Naw,' said Phoebe. 'My mom says we have to say we're sorry for calling you a freak, 'cause you're not. Sorry.'

'Sorry,' Jane added.

Jack thought for a moment and then said, 'It's OK.'

'Want a Twinkie?' asked Phoebe as she knelt down and opened her lunch box.

'My mom says I can't eat other people's food,' Jack answered with disappointment.

'So?' Phoebe asked.

Jack paused and decided to take the Twinkie after all. He tore off the wrapper as he walked away.

Phoebe and Jane ran after Jack. Phoebe tugged at his jacket.

'You must have been born in a leap year, mister,' Phoebe said, catching her breath.

'No, and don't call me "mister",' answered Jack while trying to swallow a mouthful of Twinkie.

'Every four years is your birthday. You've only had ten birthdays because of –' Phoebe continued.

Jane cut her off. 'Nuh-uh. If he was born in a leap year he would have had only four birthdays but he would still look . . . ten. Or something.'

'But I'm eight. And I don't look nearly as old as you. I mean, come on.' Phoebe looked confused.

'You will when you're ten,' Jack said, giggling.

'That's a joke, right?' Jane asked anxiously.

'I was born in September,' Jack told them.

'If he was born in a leap year, he would only have had ten birthdays but he would look forty, like he does . . .' Phoebe tried to explain to Jane.

'Yeah, right, it's like *Star Trek*,' Jane said as she pulled a long strand of hair out of her mouth.

'Nuh-uh, 'cause it's real,' Phoebe disagreed.

'Stop!' yelled Jane.

'You stop!' yelled Phoebe.

Jack rolled his eyes and walked away from the girls. He found a kerb to sit down on and looked around the playground. He remembered he had a bag of Gummi Bear sweets in his jacket pocket. He pulled out the bag and tore it open. Jack then noticed that right next to his big trainers stood a pair of black high-heeled pumps. His eyes followed the pumps up to the legs, up to the dress, up to the face. It was Miss Marquez.

'How are you doing, Jack?' she asked him.

'Hi, Miss Marquez.' Jack tried to smile without revealing the mutilated Gummi Bear in his mouth.

'May I?' asked Miss Marquez, pointing to the sweets.

Jack held out the open bag to his teacher. He smiled and played with one shoelace.

'Could I get a red one?' she asked. 'The red ones are my favourite.' Miss Marquez stuck her hand in the bag and pulled out a little red Gummi Bear. Jack noticed how she sucked on it instead of chewing it.

Miss Marquez stood and talked with Jack for a while longer. Their conversation was interrupted by two girls singing.

'Miss Marquez and Jack, sitting in a tree. K-I-S-S-I-N-G. First comes love, then comes marriage . . .' It was Phoebe and Jane. They were standing behind a tree, laughing as they sang.

Jack's face turned the same colour as a red Gummi Bear, listening to them sing. But Miss Marquez reassured Jack that everything was OK and not to worry. Then she walked over towards the girls to reprimand them.

'Hey, thanks for lunch,' Miss Marquez called back to Jack.

7
The Game of His Life

JACK HAD A warm feeling inside him as he continued walking through the playground. He was thinking about Miss Marquez and how nice she was. Jack thought that he was so lucky to have such a kind and understanding teacher – and one who loves Gummi Bears. He reached into his bag of sweets, pulled out a green bear and popped it into his mouth. While he picked the sticky sweet from his teeth, he noticed Louis and his buddies standing by the basketball court.

'Let's go Louis-er. To ten,' shouted Victor as he and a bunch of his tough friends charged on to the court.

Louis watched Victor stand in front of him and dribble the basketball. He wasn't in the mood to play ball with Victor, but sometimes with Victor

41

you didn't have much of a choice. Louis looked over to John John to see what he thought.

'I'm not in the mood to get my butt kicked today,' John John told Louis.

'Well,' said Louis, 'we've got the new kid.' Louis pointed over to the other side of the court where Jack was standing.

Everything was quiet. All of Louis's friends' mouths dropped open. They couldn't believe their ears!

'You can't pick him. He can't play with us,' demanded Victor.

'I can pick whoever I want. Whattaya, afraid to lose?' asked Louis with a smirk on his face.

'No!' shouted Eric. 'Pick whoever you want. We never lose.'

Louis turned towards Jack. 'Hey you, big guy,' he called. 'You shoot hoops?'

'Me?' Jack gulped. He turned and looked behind him to make sure that Louis was really talking to him.

'No, the other forty-year-old kid behind you,' said Louis as he rolled his eyes. 'You play ball?'

'A little,' answered Jack in a meek voice.

Louis's friends were incredulous. They thought their buddy had really lost it this time.

John John asked Louis, 'Are you fried?'

'At least nobody's going to slam him,' said Louis as he walked on to the basketball court.

John John and his friends shrugged their shoulders and followed Louis to the court. Jack followed too – about ten paces behind. Jack was about to take part in a game that would change his life.

Everyone was gathered on the court. Victor held on to the ball. 'Who's that,' he asked Louis, 'your mascot?'

'Maybe we can use him for a hoop,' added Eric. Then he turned to Jack and said, 'Make a circle with your hands and act like a pole.'

'Yeah,' said another kid named Mario. 'His head looks like a backboard.'

Right then, Victor threw the ball at Jack. The ball caught Jack off guard. It bounced off his chest and Louis grabbed it.

'Loser takes out. So you guys take out,' Victor ordered.

The game began. Everyone took their positions on the court. Jack stood on the sidelines waiting for Louis to throw him the ball, but Victor intercepted it. Jack panicked and backed away from Victor. Victor scored, and Jack let out a deep sigh of disappointment for Louis and his gang of friends.

'Invincible,' Victor called out with his arms up in the air.

'This is gonna be bad,' George muttered to himself.

Louis took the ball out again. He threw it to John John, who then got the ball stolen from him by Eric. Eric held the ball up, about to shoot, when Jack grabbed it out of his hands. Jack looked for someone to pass to, but all his teammates were blocked. So from right across the court, Jack decided to shoot the ball. He took a deep breath and . . . *swoosh*, he scored! Everyone on Jack's team cheered.

'Loser takes out,' Louis said, smiling as he threw the ball over to Victor.

The game continued. Victor passed the ball to Eric. Eric dribbled for a while then fumbled. The ball landed back in Victor's hands. He tried to get past Jack but couldn't. Jack stole the ball and, once again, scored from across the court.

'Yes!' Louis cried out.

'First time we've ever been up by two,' John

John said excitedly. He turned to Jack. 'Way to go, big guy.'

Jack was beaming. Then he noticed that he and his team-mates had an audience. A crowd of kids stood on the sidelines, engrossed in the game. Even Miss Marquez looked excited.

Victor was so mad he could barely stand it. He came up with a plan. He passed the ball to one of his team-mates and gave a sign to Eric. Then Victor and Eric headed over to where Jack was. They tried to block him. But the ball ended up in Jack's hands anyway, and before Victor or Eric had a chance to see what was happening, Jack had made yet another basket.

'Six–two! Unstoppable!' George called out as he jumped up and down.

'Like this is fair,' said Victor, wiping the sweat off his face.

From the crowd came cheers. Kids called out Jack's name. Jack was a hit! Louis walked over to Jack and jumped up next to him with his hand out. He was giving Jack a high five. It was the first high five that Jack had ever received. This was a day Jack would always remember.

8
Principal Jack

Later in the day, Jack sat at his big desk on his big chair in Miss Marquez's class. He was grinning from ear to ear. It was Friday and the school day was nearly over, but all Jack could think about was the basketball game. Jack's thoughts were interrupted by the sound of his teacher's voice.

'We have a new assignment – something I want you to put some thought into. I would like you all to write an essay on what you want to be when you grow up. Be sure to include reasons for your choices. You have until the end of the term to finish it.'

'I wanna be a gynaecologist,' George called out.

'George, think before you speak. This will be

a big part of your grade,' Miss Marquez said sternly.

Miss Marquez walked past Jack's desk and bent down to whisper something to him.

'Nice shooting today, Jack,' she said. 'Way to go.'

Jack's heart skipped a beat! He responded to Miss Marquez's warm smile, staring into her eyes with adoration.

A few moments later the school bell rang. All the kids rushed out of the classrooms and to the front of the school, looking for their lifts home. Louis stood in front of the school saying goodbye to all of his friends. But he didn't go home. He was looking for Jack. Then Louis spotted him.

'Hey, nice game today,' Louis called out to get Jack's attention.

'Thanks.' Jack nodded.

Louis ran over to Jack and said, 'Now you gotta do me another favour.'

'What is it?' Jack asked as he wrinkled up his eyebrows.

Louis grabbed the sleeve of Jack's jacket and said, 'Follow me.'

He led Jack around the side of the school to an out-of-the-way place where no one could see them.

'What are we doing here?' Jack asked. He now felt a little nervous.

'Listen,' Louis began. 'My mother's coming here to meet the principal today. She wants to talk to him.'

'Yeah.' Jack looked at him blankly.

'Well, you're gonna be the principal.'

'Huh … what?' Jack asked as he started to walk away from Louis.

'You gotta do it,' Louis begged. 'If my mom talks to Principal McGee, he'll tell her that I've been bad.'

'Have you been bad?' Jack asked.

'I haven't done homework since, like, the third grade,' Louis answered seriously.

'Boy, your dog must be really full.' Jack giggled as he said that.

'Yeah, right.' Louis laughed too. As his mother's car pulled up to the front of the building, Louis became even more anxious. 'Here she is. You gotta do it.'

'Louis, I can't be a principal,' Jack tried to convince his new friend, but it was too late. Louis was already dragging him over to where his mother was standing.

Louis's mother stood on the pavement. She had

red hair piled high on top of her head and a bright, thick coat of make-up on her face. She wore a tight black skirt and a leopard-skin patterned jacket.

'Hi, Ma. This is Principal Powell,' said Louis. 'He's new here. He just came a couple of weeks ago. I told him you were coming.'

'Hi, Mr Powell. My name's Dolores. Friends call me DD. What happened to Principal McGee? I just spoke to him.'

Jack was frozen. He was sweating, not knowing what to say. 'Oh. He got diarrhoea,' he blurted out.

Louis kicked Jack in the leg. He couldn't believe the pathetic excuse his friend had come up with.

'Diarrhoea?' asked Dolores. She thought that sounded very strange.

'Yeah . . . a bellyache,' Jack added.

'He had to go to the hospital . . . appendicitis,' Louis said, thinking that made it sound legitimate.

Louis's mum seemed to believe the lie. She told Louis to walk away so she could talk with Principal Powell alone. Louis pleaded with his mother to let him stay, but she wouldn't have it.

'See, that's the problem – he doesn't listen,' Dolores told Jack about her son. 'Isn't that the trouble with most kids?' She looked to Jack to see what his thoughts were on the subject.

'What did you say?' replied Jack.

'I said most kids don't listen.' She looked bewildered.

'Don't listen,' Jack said, pausing for a moment. 'Yeah,' he responded.

'That's what I thought. Actually, it's the problem with most men. Am I right? Your wife probably says that to you.' Dolores smiled.

'No,' he said.

'Are you married?' Dolores asked Jack.

'Married. No, not married,' said Jack matter-of-factly.

Hearing this made Dolores's face light up. She became excited with the idea of possibly dating a principal.

'I'm divorced myself,' she explained. 'That's why I'm having so much trouble with Louis. His father left a few years ago, and since that time, he's had a chip on his shoulder.'

'Oh, that must hurt,' Jack replied as he played with the good-luck rabbit-foot keyring that was in his pocket.

Dolores laughed. 'And he's at that age when he's starting to think about girls,' she continued. 'I found some dirty magazines under his bed.'

'It's a tough age. I know . . . I mean, I remember it well. I mean, I'm remembering it well. Tough age. Rough, tough.' Jack fumbled with his words as he tried desperately to pull this principal thing off for the sake of his new friend.

Louis was pretty impressed with how Jack was doing. He stood several feet away from where Jack and his mum were talking, and he was straining his ears so as not to miss a word that was being said. He caught Jack's eye and gave him a thumbs-up sign. Jack continued to talk with Dolores Durante and lay the lies on thicker and thicker.

'Louis is one of the best students in the whole school,' he told Dolores. 'Maybe even the smartest kid I ever met.'

'Really?' Louis's mother hadn't dreamed of hearing these words from a principal! 'Well, I am surprised, but that's great to hear. Maybe we could have lunch and talk more about this.' She threw Jack a very sweet smile.

When Louis heard what his mum said, he was so embarrassed. His mother had a habit of trying very hard to impress most single men with whom she came into contact. He had to cut into the conversation before Dolores went too far. Louis walked over to where his mum and Jack stood.

'I hear you've been quite a good boy,' Dolores told her son.

'I told you,' he answered. Louis could not believe how well the meeting had gone!

Dolores reached her hand deep down inside her handbag. She was looking for something to write her telephone number on to give to 'Principal Powell' so he could report to her on Louis's progress. She pulled an old book of matches out of her bag and scrawled her number in the corner.

'My mom says I shouldn't touch matches,' Jack blurted out without thinking.

'You live with your mother?' Dolores questioned him. But she didn't give it much more thought.

Jack looked at the book of matches and noticed there was a name written on it in bright-red script. It said MEMORIES BAR AND GRILL.

'That's just a place I go to. If I'm not at work, I'm usually there. It's a nice place for people our age to get together, kick back a bit. Bye-bye.'

Dolores gave Jack a little wave as she walked off towards her car.

Louis quickly whispered into Jack's ear. 'Hey, man, I owe you one,' he said. 'Sorry about my mom, Jack. She's looking for love in all the wrong places.' Then Louis pulled something out of his pocket. It was the rubber eyeball Jack threw out of his window that day a few weeks ago. 'Here – want it back?' he asked.

'No, you keep it.' Jack was delighted that Louis had held on to the toy for so long in the first place.

'Maybe I'll see you over the weekend,' Louis told Jack, and then ran over to his mum.

9
When Jack Grows Up

JACK LEFT SCHOOL that day with the most exhilarated feeling he had ever had! He ran the entire way home and didn't even have to stop once to catch his breath! He felt as though he were a kite floating on air, because his feet barely touched the ground. But unlike a kite, he wasn't floating aimlessly. He was heading straight home so he could share stories of his amazing day with his parents.

He zipped down Forest Lane and turned the corner on to Beechwood Drive. Jack was almost home. He ran up the driveway to his house and threw open the kitchen door.

'Maaa, I'm home!' Jack called out. He pulled off his jacket and kicked off his trainers. Jack yanked open the refrigerator door and poured himself a tall glass of orange juice. He picked up the telephone and began to dial Brian's work number.

Just then Karen walked into the kitchen and was thrilled to see her son's face beaming with excitement. She compared his look to the day before and noted his miraculous mood change. She listened to Jack talk to his dad on the phone.

'I played basketball with these kids,' he was saying. 'I scored a thousand points . . . No, you're right, it was a hundred . . . No, I'm kidding . . . It was great. I met this kid, Louis. His mom gave me matches. Can I play with them? Louis has dirty magazines under his bed . . .' Jack went on telling his father about the highlights of the day. 'I pretended to be the principal,' he continued. 'I got homework I gotta do . . . And this Miss Marquez said, "Way to go," and patted me on the shoulder, and then she ate a Gummi Bear . . . Not a bad day, no.'

Jack rambled on until finally Brian told him that he would see him when he got home from work.

Jack replaced the receiver and grabbed a few biscuits to take to his room. He plopped down on his bed, opened his notebook, and read his homework assignment.

What do I want to be when I grow up? A basketball player or maybe a doctor. A salesman, a lawyer, a policeman, a comedian . . . a principal! He laughed, remembering his encounter with Louis's mother. The truth was, Jack had no idea what he wanted to be. He drew a big question mark in his notebook and then closed it.

The following day was Saturday. Karen and Jack were playing one of their favourite games: Laser Warriors. Karen wore a thick mask and held a big, plastic gun in her hand. She ran after Jack, who wore a metallic silver mask and outfit. They looked like they belonged in some cheap futuristic film. Karen pulled the trigger on her toy gun, which made loud noises that sounded like a car alarm. They were making too much noise and having too much fun to realize that someone was ringing the doorbell.

It was Louis who stood frustrated at the Powells' front door. He heard noises coming from inside the house, and he was eager to talk with his new friend.

'Hey, Jack! Hey, Jack's mother!' he screamed

after realizing that the bell was doing him no good.

Finally Karen came to the door. Louis stared at her standing there in her strange costume. He was a little nervous until she pulled off her mask and revealed her face.

'Jack's mother, can Jack come out and play?' he asked.

'I'm Mrs Powell. And you're . . . ?' Karen looked down at Louis while she waited for an answer.

'Louis Durante,' he said. 'Pleased to meet you. I know Jack from school. I was wondering if Jack wanted to come to a sleepover some of us guys are having. I mean, if he's allowed and stuff.'

While Karen thought about whether it was OK if Jack left for the night, Jack came running down the stairs carrying a bag. He was all packed and ready to go.

'Bye, Ma, see ya!' he called as he hopped on his bicycle.

Karen watched as her son rode away with his friend. Jack carried his duffel bag slung over one shoulder. She noticed a toothbrush sticking out of one back pocket and a comb sticking out of the other.

'Don't stay up late,' she called to him. 'And be careful! Call me with the phone number.' Karen stood on the front porch for several minutes after Jack rode away. This was the first time Jack would be spending a night away from home.

10

Just One of the Guys

JACK AND LOUIS arrived at John John's house.
They rode their bikes up the driveway and
parked them beside the front porch next to all
the other bicycles. John John's house was white
with pale-blue trim and there were toys strewn
all around the front porch.

Behind the house, Jack noticed what he thought
was an odd-looking structure at first. But as he
got closer to it, he realized it was a humongous
tree house! The house was built up high in an
old oak tree. Jack's jaw dropped open at the sight
of it. From inside the tree house, he heard the
sound of boys laughing. How cool, Jack thought
to himself. But as they got closer, he became
apprehensive.

Louis entered the tree through a knothole in

the oak's enormous trunk. He looked back down at Jack as he began to climb up the stairway that was built inside the tree.

'Don't sweat it,' Louis told Jack. 'Just go along with whatever I say.'

'You think the other kids are going to like me?' Jack asked nervously as he started up the stairs.

'You're tight with me, you're tight with them,' Louis said reassuringly. 'They're going to love you!' he promised. Louis pushed open the small trapdoor at the base of the tree house.

'You brought the freak!' John John blurted out immediately.

Jack felt sick. Should he run back down the stairs and out of the tree? Should he go back home? But he couldn't move. He did what he always did when he was nervous, remained still – as frozen as an icicle. Fortunately, his friend stood up for him.

'He's not a freak!' Louis demanded. 'He's cool – he knows how to shoot hoops, and he did me a favour. And check this out. Look what he picked up on the way over.' Louis pulled out a magazine from his bag and handed it to John John.

John John looked at the cover of the magazine. It was an adult magazine.

'He bought that? No way,' John John said.

'Way. He walked right into the store and picked it up. No fear, no nothing. My man's the man,' Louis said proudly.

'That is way cool,' George said excitedly, and he grabbed the magazine out of John John's hands.

'Wish I was a freak,' Edward said while eating a handful of cheese snacks.

'Lay off the freak stuff.' Louis was already annoyed. 'Jack's all right, and we've got to let him kick it with us. If he walks, the magazine walks too.'

No one seemed to like the idea of losing the magazine.

'OK, he can hang,' said John John. 'But if he weirds out or anything, he's history.'

'Wait a second,' Edward interjected. 'We'll exceed maximum weight up here. I don't think this is a good idea.'

But this didn't impress Louis. He waved his hand at Edward. Anyway, Edward was the nervous type. He always found something to worry about. Louis went to get Jack, who was anxiously waiting on the stairs in the tree trunk.

'You're in. Come on up,' Louis said, smiling.

Jack nodded then walked up the last few steps and squeezed himself through the trapdoor. He made it into the tree house and knelt on the floor as he took everything in. He saw the guys. Edward, John John, and George all stared at him. He noticed all the posters on the walls and the piles of junk-food wrappers that were all over the floor.

'Guys, this is Jack,' Louis said to break the moment of silence.

Jack waved to the guys and they waved back. Then Jack stood up and hit his head on the ceiling. He lost his balance and ended up knocking a poster off the wall. He made a mental note to himself to remember to duck the next time he was in the tree house.

'You bought that magazine?' George asked. He was still thinking about how cool that was.

Jack was caught a bit off guard because the fact was, he hadn't bought that magazine at all. Louis had found the magazine in the rubbish that morning, but thought it would be a way for the guys to accept Jack if they believed that he was the one who bought it. Jack caught Louis's eye and went along with the story.

'Yeah, I did,' he said nonchalantly. 'I buy 'em all the time,' he added.

Jack went on to convince the guys that he could buy any magazine at all.

'The cashiers don't ask for any ID?' George was bewildered.

'No, I just don't shave for a day, and then they think I'm, like, fifty.' Jack chuckled, and everyone laughed along with him. Jack sighed with relief as he realized things were loosening up.

'So, what's up with the way you look?' asked Edward as he licked some orange crumbs off his upper lip. 'I mean, Miss Marquez said you're the same age as us, but you look like my Uncle Solomon.'

'He ages faster than us,' Louis explained. 'Is that cool or what?'

All the guys agreed that was pretty cool. George leafed through the magazine, and Edward scooted over to sit next to Jack.

'You really shave, Jack?' Edward looked closely at Jack's face, checking out his razor stubble.

'Started when I was four,' Jack answered proudly.

'I'm looking forward to shaving. Whattaya think, you see anything there?' He put his face up close to Jack. 'Any whiskers?' he asked in a hopeful voice.

'Man, if I were you, I'd grow, like, a Fu Manchu thing or a goatee. It would be the coolest thing.'

Louis walked over to where his giant friend was sitting. 'So, how do you like it?' he asked, referring to the tree house.

Jack took another long look around him. He looked at all the posters on the wall again. There were women in bathing suits, an image of a basketball player doing a slam dunk, an aerial view of a baseball diamond. He noticed stacks of baseball cards piled high on a little card table. Underneath the table were empty cans of soda and half-empty packets of biscuits. Jack loved everything about the tree house. Louis could tell by Jack's expression that he thought the place was great.

'So what do you guys do here all night?' Jack asked the gang.

'Anything we want.' George smiled.

*　　*　　*

In the Powell house, Karen sat on her son's bed. She missed Jack. She looked across the room and spotted the big cardboard box that Jack loved to play in. Karen walked over to the box and decided to sit in it. Just then, Brian walked into Jack's room. He had heard sounds from there and had wondered what they were.

'Jack?' Brian said.

'No, it's me,' said Karen shyly from inside the box.

Brian smiled as he poked his head into the box to see his wife. Then Brian decided to join his wife in the big box. So he climbed in too.

'It's only . . . you know, this is where we usually talk before bed,' Karen explained.

'And you feel traded in for a bunch of spitting, swearing ten-year-olds?' Brian asked half kiddingly. 'It's just the way it is for everybody,' he continued. 'You give birth to them, you clothe them, feed them. Then one day you come home, they're teenagers, they hate you for no reason, and they wouldn't talk to you if your hair was on fire.'

'I know. He's never spent the night away before, that's all.' Karen gave her husband a look that said, I know I'm being silly, but I just can't help it.

'We've never been alone in this house before,' Brian said to Karen and he snuggled closer to her and kissed her on the cheek. 'I think it's nice to be the only size-eleven shoes under our bed.'

While Karen and Brian adjusted to the quiet in their house, Jack was having a blast with all his new friends in the tree house.

Jack and his pals were in the middle of a contest, and it looked as though Jack was going to be the winner. He held an empty coffee jar up to his rear end as the guys cheered him on.

'I wanna hear a good one,' yelled Edward above the laughs and snorts from the other guys. 'A good manly rip. Show us what you're made of.'

At that moment, Jack let it rip.

'Rip-roaring. The earth is rumbling!' Louis said.

'Jack Powell. Unbelievable ability!' added Edward.

'Pass it down. George has to smell it to see if it was lethal,' said John John, motioning for the coffee jar.

Jack brought the jar over to George. The lid was on so as not to let out any of the noxious fumes. He put the jar up to George's nose and removed the lid. George gasped. He fell backwards, pretending to pass out from the smell. Everyone laughed hysterically.

Once the contest came to an end, it was time to initiate Jack into the tree house as a member. He sat next to three bowls of food with a blindfold covering his eyes. He reached his hand into the first bowl of food. It was filled with grapes.

'Ugh. Eyeballs,' Jack said.

Then he put his hand into the next bowl. That bowl was filled with cold spaghetti.

'Worms, maggots. Yuk!' he exclaimed.

Then Jack put his hand into the third bowl. In that bowl were pieces of cut-up bananas. Jack thought they felt like guts.

Jack took off the blindfold and continued with the initiation. In front of him sat a giant-sized piece of chocolate cake drenched in mayonnaise, relish, ketchup, and mustard. To top it off, there were a few sprinkles of Tabasco sauce on it.

Jack eyed the cake and grabbed his belly.

'I can't do it. I can't do it. I can't do it,' he kept repeating out loud.

Louis carried the cake over to Jack and placed the plate in his hands.

'I can't eat it.' Jack felt sick already.

The gang cheered him on. 'Go, go, go, go,' they all chanted.

Jack lifted up his fork and got himself a big piece of cake smothered in a mound of the mayonnaise, relish, ketchup, mustard and hot sauce. He opened his mouth wide to receive the pile of disgusting mush and . . . he ate it all up!

'That was good,' he said as he let out an enormous belch.

The gang was definitely impressed.

It was close to one o'clock in the morning, and the gang's energy seemed to be petering out. They were all lying in their sleeping bags, trying to fight off sleep.

Edward grabbed a stick of gum from his knapsack.

'Ain't nothing like a fresh piece of gum right before bed,' he said as he shoved the gum into his mouth and started to chomp away.

Jack had a big smile on his face. He was never as contented as he was at that moment – hanging out with his friends and just simply being one of the guys.

'Hey, you know what?' Louis asked. 'Jack's got the hots for Marquez.'

'Do not!' Jack demanded. He was so embarrassed.

'Do so. I saw you checking her out,' Louis said teasingly.

'Miss Marquez is sexy,' George said.

'I don't have the hots for her. She's our teacher – she's all old,' Jack said, trying to convince everyone.

'You're all old,' said George.

'She's old for real,' explained Jack.

'So? It's like you're the same, sort of. You should take her to the school dance,' Louis said, thinking that made perfect sense.

Jack thought a bit and then closed his eyes along with the rest of the gang. And then in the dark, and finally quiet, tree house, John John spoke.

'Hey, you know, Jack, you're all right. You're really not dangerous at all,' he said.

'Just wait till you're sleeping, John John,' Louis said. 'That's when he eats children. Right, Jack?' he sniggered.

'That's right.' Jack laughed along with Louis. He then closed his eyes once more and drifted off to sleep.

*   *   *

During the days following Jack's initial visit to the tree house, he had the time of his life. He hung out with the gang, and for the first time Jack felt like he really fitted in.

He would walk down the corridors in school with Louis, Edward, John John, and George at his side, and no one would dare pick on him – not even Eric or Victor. He became even better at shooting hoops. There was just no stopping him on the basketball court, and he was becoming a pretty good football player too!

One afternoon, Jack decided to introduce his new buddies to one of his dearest friends, Mr Woodruff. He brought Mr Woodruff over to the tree house.

'This is Mr Woodruff,' said Jack as he held the trapdoor open so Mr Woodruff could squeeze through.

'Are you ten too?' asked Edward as he chomped away on a stick of gum.

'Well, if you talk to my wife . . . but no,' joked Mr Woodruff, 'I'm just a regular garden-variety old guy.'

The guys were disappointed to hear this. They were hoping to meet someone else just like their friend Jack.

My Woodruff ended up being pretty cool himself. He went through the entire initiation procedure that Jack had gone through. The guys cheered Mr Woodruff on as he put a spoonful of a truly revolting combination of foods into his mouth. He swallowed the peanut butter, cottage cheese, tuna fish, chocolate syrup and garlic. He took a deep breath to try to fight the urge to throw up.

'Way to go, Woody, my man,' Jack said as he exchanged high fives with the guys. The boys cheered wildly. They were definitely impressed with him.

Mr Woodruff hung out with his young pals in the tree house for the afternoon. He told them stories about himself and what it was like for him growing up. Everyone told jokes; Mr Woodruff told some very corny ones. He put a cassette of music that he listened to when he was a kid into the tape player. The gang had a hysterical time singing along to the music with Mr Woodruff.

As everyone belted out tunes from the past, something bizarre was happening. The tree house was vibrating! It started to rock slowly back and forth, back and forth, and then there was a rumbling noise. No one heard the noise over all the singing that was going on. Then the tree house actually shifted. The only one who began to notice that something was not right was Edward.

'Wait a second! Wait a second!' he screamed over the singing. 'Shut up! Shut up!'

One by one, they stopped singing and looked at Edward like he was crazy until they heard the rumbling themselves.

'We're at the absolute limit of this structure,' Edward said in a panicked voice.

'There's nothing wrong, Eddie. You're paranoid.' John John waved his hand at his friend, figuring nothing horrible could happen.

Just then a tiny, beautiful butterfly flew into the tree house. It was yellow with pretty blue-and-green marks on its wings. All the guys noticed the butterfly and watched it fly around the room. Then, ever so slowly, it circled the window and made its descent on to the window sill. Then the fort shook uncontrollably. It rumbled and swayed. '*Aaaaggghhh*,' everyone screamed at the top of their lungs. They were going down and they knew it! The house tumbled downwards and landed with an enormous *thud* on the ground. Screams filled John John's back garden, when all of a sudden they noticed they'd hit the ground.

'I told you so,' Edward said to his friends, chewing nervously on his gum.

11

Love in the Air

J ACK WOKE UP to the sound of his clock radio. He noticed that it was a beautiful day as he quickly glanced out the window on the way to the bathroom. The sun was shining, and the birds were chirping. The feeling of love was definitely in the air.

Jack stood in front of the bathroom mirror grooming himself. He lathered up with foamy shaving-cream and took the razor to his face like an old pro. Jack stared directly into the mirror and thought long and hard about his hair. He brushed it to the left and then to the right and then straight back. He wasn't happy. Then he noticed a bunch of strands of his hair in the sink. He looked at his scalp and saw that his hairline was even higher than it had been a few months

Mr Woodruff, Jack's tutor, approaches his whimpering pupil. He tells him the best way to heal a scuffed knee is to bite it!

Jack creates his own war games in the back garden.

Celebrating his tenth birthday, Jack's about to make a very important wish!

Jack gently balances a butterfly on his finger.

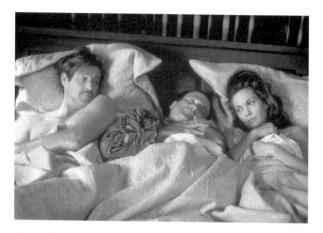

Snuggling between Mum and Dad, Jack feels safe at last!

Jack's first day of school is not easy. He sits on the kerb in the playground feeling very lonely.

Two girls, Phoebe and Jane, poke and inspect Jack. They can't believe he's actually their age!

Armed with space-age squirt guns, Jack and his mum prepare for battle.

Jack hangs out with his new friends in John John's tree house.

With John John on his back and the other kids executing a tackle, Jack races to the end zone.

Victory!

Jack plays around at the gang's tree house.

The foundations of the fort rumble and shake – then it begins to collapse!

Jack, Mr Woodruff and the rest of the gang tumble into a big, messy heap.

ago. He was trying to touch it up with some of his father's black shoe polish when he heard his mother's voice from downstairs.

'Jack, it's eight-fifteen! You're cutting it close!' she called.

Jack took another look at himself in the mirror and slapped some aftershave on his face. His hair would have to do. Jack ran downstairs into the kitchen and grabbed two blueberry muffins and his bag, and went off to school.

During lunch break, Jack and Louis were hanging out in the school playground looking for a girl named Lucy. Louis had a crush on her. Lucy had shoulder-length, curly, golden-brown hair. Her eyes were deep green and she had just a few freckles scattered across the bridge of her small nose.

Louis elbowed Jack. He wanted Jack to go up to Lucy and convince her to go to the school dance with Louis. Louis was too shy to do it himself. Jack walked over to Lucy, and as he approached her he gave Louis an OK sign from behind his back.

'Hi, Lucy.' Jack smiled at the petite girl wearing a denim dress.

'Hi, Jack.' Lucy smiled back at him. 'What are you doing?' she asked innocently.

'Nothing,' Jack quickly replied. 'Guess what?' he said.

'What?'

'Somebody thinks you're cute. His initials are L.D. Want another hint?' asked Jack.

'No,' replied Lucy as she looked to the side of Jack and noticed Louis standing in the distance.

'He's, like, shy, you know? But he's totally cool and everything. He's got, like, Sega, and a pool and . . .' Jack thought for a moment. 'And, uh, he can get girlie magazines.'

'So?' Lucy asked, a bit confused.

'And, he's not going to the dance with anyone,' added Jack.

'If he wants to ask me to the dance then why doesn't he ask me?' said Lucy as she began to walk away.

'Like I said, he's shy,' Jack explained while he walked next to Lucy. 'And . . . you should hear him let off!'

Lucy scrunched up her little nose so it had about fifteen tiny wrinkles on it. She was completely disgusted by Jack's comment.

'No, it's cool,' Jack tried desperately to convince her. 'And he can blow soda through his nose . . .' Jack looked over his shoulder and saw Louis standing in the distance, biting his fingernails. Jack said goodbye to Lucy and went back over to his friend.

'What happened? What happened?' Louis asked anxiously.

'She said she'd like to get to know you a little bit,' Jack began. 'Maybe speak to you once or twice, you know.'

'She said no,' Louis said. He seemed upset.

'No. Not no. Not anything,' Jack tried to make his buddy feel hopeful. 'It's still open for business. You just gotta work it.'

Louis sighed and then asked Jack what plans he had for asking someone to the dance.

'I got some ideas,' Jack said, and then he gave his friend a reassuring pat on the back. Then they headed back to class.

Everyone in Miss Marquez's class sat at their desks with their notebooks open. Miss Marquez asked a few kids to read their essay about what they wanted to be when they grew up.

At this point, Jack was deep in thought. His essay wasn't ready, and he still didn't have any idea what he was going to write. He knew something was keeping him from writing the essay. Jack doodled on a piece of paper. Then he wrote down the number 28. He then multiplied that number by four and came up with 112. Jack felt as if he had a gigantic knot in his stomach. His eyes were fixed on that 112, for that's how old he would look when he was only twenty-eight years old!

The school bell rang to signal the end of the day, but Jack's eyes were still fixed on the numbers in front of him. He wasn't exactly sure how he felt, but he knew it wasn't a good feeling. This was something that he had thought about lots of times before today, but it had never had the same impact on him as it did right then in Miss Marquez's classroom.

Louis tried to get his buddy Jack to walk out of school with him, but Jack refused. He told Louis that he needed to talk with Miss Marquez about something. Louis just shrugged his shoulders and told Jack that he would wait for him at the front of the school.

Jack was the only one left in the classroom – except for Miss Marquez, that is. She looked perfect to Jack. He gazed at her while she gathered papers on her desk and organized her briefcase. He was so taken by her beauty that he could barely breathe.

Miss Marquez looked up from what she was doing and was surprised to see that Jack was still in the room.

'Jack, you're still here?' she asked. Then Miss Marquez noticed that Jack looked a bit strange. His face was flushed and he was sweating profusely. And right around his hairline, the tiny beads of sweat that were forming were black. The shoe polish had turned the sweat black! 'Jack, what's wrong? You feel OK?' she asked in a very concerned voice.

Jack took a deep breath and approached Miss Marquez. He held out a bag of sweets. 'I know you like 'em, so I saved you all the red Gummi Bears,' he said as he handed her the bag.

'That's so sweet of you, Jack,' Miss Marquez said, smiling widely.

'I'm a nice guy, huh?' Jack asked.

'You're a very nice young man,' replied his teacher.

Now Jack took an even deeper breath. 'I was thinking that maybe, if you weren't doing anything, that, um, you might want to go to the dance with me. It would be really, really, fun.'

'Oh, Jackie . . .' she said sweetly.

'So, you want to go? My mom could drive us,' Jack asked hopefully.

'I don't think you'd want me to go with you. I'm an old lady.' Miss Marquez was trying to be as tactful as possible.

'That's OK. I can't go with girls my age 'cause I look older than them, but you look old like me,' Jack said, thinking his reasoning made perfect sense. 'So what time do you want me and my mom to pick you up?'

'Jack, you're my pupil, and I'm your teacher, and teachers aren't supposed to go with pupils to dances.' Miss Marquez tried to find just the right words to say to Jack. 'It . . . it just wouldn't be . . .'

Jack was heartbroken. He turned away from Miss Marquez and headed for the classroom door. He walked out of the room and started sprinting down the corridor.

Miss Marquez called to him, 'Are you all right, honey? Come back – let's talk.'

'NO! I don't want to talk! Just leave me alone!' he screamed.

Jack ran faster and faster down the corridor. Tears welled up in his eyes and began to roll down his face. He could barely see through all the tears in his eyes. When Jack reached the staircase, he leaped down the steps two at a time, sometimes even three. When Jack reached the bottom of the staircase he could hardly catch his breath. Something was wrong. He felt a sharp pain in his chest, grabbed his shirt near his heart, and fell to the floor.

Louis was standing outside near the staircase when he heard a huge thud. He ran inside to find his best friend in the entire world practically crumpled up in a ball at the bottom of the stairs!

'Jack, Jack!' Louis screamed. 'Someone help us!'

12

An Aching Heart

KAREN AND BRIAN Powell ran down the corridor of St Vincent's Hospital, frantically trying to find their son. They stopped a nurse, and she showed the Powells to Jack's room.

Jack lay on a hospital stretcher with his eyes closed. There were so many wires connecting him to so many monitors and machines that he almost looked like a machine himself. Dr Benfante examined Jack. He was the very same doctor that had delivered Jack more than ten years ago.

'I think what has happened is the result of severe strain,' Dr Benfante told the Powells.

Brian, Karen, and the doctor stepped out of the room to talk.

'So it wasn't a heart attack?' Brian asked.

'Well – not exactly. This is a form of angina,

but Jack's situation is unique. His forty-year-old heart is trying desperately to keep up with his ten-year-old mind. That, combined with his rapid growth, has caused a great deal of wear and tear on his heart. His internal clock is . . . running out,' said Dr Benfante with a grim look on his face.

The following day, Jack was going to be released from the hospital. After he buttoned his shirt and washed his face, Jack walked through the hospital corridor in search of his parents. He came to a halt before he reached the door of Dr Benfante's office. He heard the voices of his parents coming from inside the office, and he stood in the corridor, listening to their conversation.

'He's beginning to experience the limitations of midlife,' Dr Benfante explained. He was continuing the conversation from the day before.

'That's not something he should have to deal with now,' remarked Brian. He ran his hands through his hair as he tried to make sense out of what was going on.

'There's no real treatment for this,' said Dr Benfante. 'Look, Brian, we don't know what Jack is going through. I can only recommend that he take it easy.'

As Jack listened intently, his heart began to hurt again. But this time it hurt in a different way. Jack was overwhelmed with sadness, so much so that his heart ached from it.

'I think it would be best if Jack stayed home for a while,' the doctor continued.

Jack wasn't surprised to hear this, but still he was crushed. School was the best thing that had happened to him for a long time. Jack was terrified of losing that.

Jack, Karen, and Brian left the hospital that day not saying much. On the way out the door, they ran into Miss Marquez. Jack could hardly look at his teacher's face. He was so embarrassed. Jack was just certain that his entire body was bright red.

'How is he?' Miss Marquez asked Karen and Brian.

'He's just fine,' Brian answered quickly.

'Brian, take Jack to the car. I'll catch up.' Karen watched her husband and son walk away, and then she turned to Miss Marquez.

'I can see what happened – I have eyes,' Karen said. 'Now I know why he's been living on Gummi Bears.'

'Everything happened so quickly,' said Miss Marquez. 'I thought it was just an innocent schoolboy crush. It happens every year,' she said, thinking this would make Karen feel better.

'Really? Every year you have a ten-year-old boy in a forty-year-old's body develop a crush on you?' asked Karen sarcastically.

'If anything like this happens again, I'll call you immediately.' Miss Marquez held tightly on to her handbag as she spoke.

'That won't be necessary. Jack won't be coming back to school. Goodbye, Miss Marquez,' said Karen, and she stomped out the door.

Jack sat on his bed that night and stared out the window. It was very dark out. The sky was a bluish black colour, but there were a few bright stars illuminating it. On Jack's lap sat his favourite stuffed animal, a very soft, tan-coloured bear wearing a red bow tie. He held his bear tightly and thought about his future. Then Jack got off of the bed and walked over to his desk. He picked up a piece of paper with the number he had computed in class the day before: 112. He sighed and turned when he heard a knock on the door. Karen entered his room.

'How are you feeling, Jackie?' Karen asked.

'I'm OK,' answered Jack in a very low voice.

Karen handed her son a large glass of juice and some cheese and crackers . . .

'Louis just called,' she said. 'He hopes you feel better. I told him you'd give him a call tomorrow. You needed some rest.'

'Why do I need rest? I feel OK,' Jack said.

'We don't want anything like this to happen again.' Karen sat down next to her son and put her arm around his shoulders. 'We'll go back to the way things were before you went to school.'

'No!' Jack shouted, and he threw himself down on his bed and buried his face in a pillow. 'No! No! No!' he yelled.

'Jackie, there isn't any other way,' Karen pleaded. She was so upset that her son was in such pain. Karen wasn't used to Jack reacting so strongly to things she said.

'But what about my friends?' asked Jack as he caught a big tear with his tongue.

'They could come by to visit,' Karen reassured Jack. 'And Mr Woodruff would come –'

'I want my friends!' demanded Jack. 'I want to go outside.'

'Honey –' Karen pleaded.

'NO!' Jack screamed and pounded the wall with his fists.

Karen started singing to her son. This usually put a smile on Jack's face, but today it didn't, work. Jack jumped off the bed and marched out of his bedroom. Karen called to him, but he wouldn't respond. He ran out of the front door to his father, who was sitting outside on the front step.

Jack ran right into his father's arms.

'Dad, Dad, don't make me stay home. I want to go back to school. Please let me go back! Don't make me be alone. Please! Please, Daddy.' Jack sobbed on his father's shoulder.

Brian just held Jack tightly and rocked him back and forth. He didn't know what he could do to ease his son's pain.

Jack stood in front of the mirror that hung above his dresser. He studied his wrinkled face in the mirror. His eyes were red and puffy from crying. He took a comb to his hair. It didn't look perfect but he didn't have the time to work on it. He dressed and quietly exited his bedroom, tiptoeing down the hallway. He stopped by his parents' bedroom door, which was open just wide enough for Jack to overhear their conversation.

'. . . afraid he'll fall down, afraid he'll hurt himself or another kid – afraid to ever have another baby . . .' said Brian to Karen.

'You know we can't do that,' Karen said sadly.

'I don't know that.'

'You know another baby might be . . .' Karen sniffled.

Jack shook his head and took several deep breaths, then he walked down the stairs and out of the house without telling his parents. Jack hopped on his bicycle and rode it quickly through the dark streets over to his school.

Jack pulled up right outside the auditorium where the school dance was taking place. He faintly heard the sound of music being played inside. Then Jack peered in the window and saw a group of kids dancing. He saw his classmates drinking punch and talking; others sat uncomfortably on benches, waiting for something to happen.

After locking his bike to a tree, Jack walked towards the school. He looked through a window in a corner of the auditorium and spotted his buddies: George was standing around eating pretzels with some other guy; Edward was chomping on gum and dancing with a girl from their class; and there was Louis, all alone, sitting on a bench, biting his fingernails. Then, out of the corner of his eye, Jack spotted Miss Marquez. He thought she looked more beautiful than ever. She had on a green dress and black shoes. She wore a strand of pearls around her neck and had one little pearl in each ear. She looked like an angel.

Jack was dying to ask Miss Marquez to dance. He pictured the scene in his head. He would tap her on the shoulder ever so gently, take her hand, and whisk her on to the dance floor. They would make the perfect pair, and everyone would stare at them as they danced the night away. But Jack's fantasy was interrupted by the heartbreaking sight of a handsome man leading Miss Marquez on to the dance floor. The two danced while Jack watched for a few minutes. Then he couldn't take it any more. His heart ached again. He walked back to his bike.

It was windy out, and rain had started to fall. Jack sat balancing himself on the seat of his bicycle, not going anywhere. He put his hand in his jacket pocket and pulled out a book of matches. It was the one that Louis's mum had given him. He saw the words written on it: MEMORIES BAR AND GRILL.

13
Jack's Big Night Out

I T WAS RAINING hard as Jack pulled into the car park lot of the Memories Bar and Grill. There was a big, gaudy sign that hung over the bar that flashed on and off in neon orange. Jack parked his bicycle and approached the door to the bar. He was sopping wet as he walked through the smoke-filled room. Although Jack was nervous and unsure of himself, he looked like he belonged.

Jack walked over to the bar and spotted an empty stool. As he squeezed his way through the crowd, he accidentally brushed someone on the side.

'Watch it,' the angry man snarled.

'Excuse me,' said Jack nervously.

The bartender walked over to where Jack was

sitting and asked him what he wanted to drink.

Jack hesitated for a moment and then said, 'I'll have a . . . Shirley Temple with extra marciano cherries.'

'Maraschino,' the bartender corrected.

'That's what I said. Maraschino,' replied Jack as he pulled on his shirt collar.

Behind Jack stood a middle-aged man. The man overheard Jack's conversation with the bartender.

'Saving the hard stuff for later?' He laughed.

'I like to start slow,' replied Jack. He smiled at his quick comeback.

'Set this guy up with one of these,' said the man as he raised his glass to the bartender. 'The name's Paulie. How's it hanging?' he asked Jack.

'OK. I'm Jack.'

When the drinks arrived, Jack gulped his down so quickly he didn't have a chance to realize how horrible it tasted.

'Here's lookin' at you, kid,' said Paulie as he guzzled his drink down too.

'I'm no kid,' said Jack defensively.

'Keep 'em coming,' Paulie called to the bartender. 'You married?' he asked Jack.

'Not yet,' he answered as he played with the tiny plastic straw in his drink.

'Lucky man. She threw me out. It's God's cruel trick, my friend. First, you lose your hair . . .' Paulie started to say.

'. . . then it shows up on your back . . .' Jack continued.

'. . . then out of your nose . . .' Paulie laughed.

'. . . and then worst of all – in your ears!' added Jack.

'Your eyebrows start growing all out of whack . . .' Paulie was laughing and snorting at this point.

'You're walking around like a bald gorilla . . .' Jack said, and then made a few ape sounds. 'You lose all your friends . . .'

'And before you know it you're pushing up daisies at some depressing cemetery, but no one comes to visit, because you cheated on your wife,' said Paulie as he wiped a tear of laughter out of the corner of his eye.

'. . . ran away from home and got your mom and dad mad at you,' Jack added.

Then Jack noticed the bar door swing open. In walked a woman wearing a leopard-print coat and puffing on a cigarette. He knew that face. It was Dolores Durante, Louis's mother. Jack stood up from the bar stool and decided to go over to Dolores.

'Go for it, Big Jack,' called Paulie.

Jack walked right up to Dolores and tapped her on the shoulder.

'Principal Powell!' she said enthusiastically. 'I can't believe you're here.'

'It's good to see someone I know.' Jack smiled.

'You wanna dance?' she asked Jack.

Jack nodded and held out his hand for Dolores. Dolores took Jack's hand and gave him a quick little smile. The two walked out on to the dance floor and started to dance. Jack felt confident. He watched the other dancers on the floor and mimicked their moves.

'You want a ciggy-butt?' asked Dolores.

Jack nodded and took a cigarette from his dance partner. He took a deep puff on it and let out a huge cough.

'I like you,' said Dolores. 'And you know who else likes you? My Louie. And he's the best judge of character, 'cause he usually doesn't like anyone that I go for. And he likes you. And I don't know, I just got a good feeling about you,' she said, smiling.

This was all getting to be too much for Jack.

'I gotta go,' he said all of a sudden. 'You're Louis's mom.' Jack turned and walked briskly through the crowded bar. Just as he passed the bar area, he knocked into the same man he had bumped earlier.

'That's the second time tonight,' yelled the man. 'What are you, stupid? I want an apology!'

'Sorry,' said Jack, and he kept walking.

'You're going to have to come up with a little more than just "sorry",' said the angry man.

'I'm sorry. Jeez, what are you, like, totally hyper or something?' asked Jack.

The man looked straight at Jack. 'You think you're pretty smart,' he said.

'In everything except social studies.' Jack giggled.

'How'd you like to study my fist?' asked the angry man as he formed a fist with his right hand, and waved it in front of Jack's face.

'You know what the problem is, mister? You have Zackly Disease.' Now Jack was really laughing.

'What's that?' asked the man.

'It means that your mouth smells ZACKLY

like your BUTT!' Jack held his belly and laughed really hard.

Dolores saw what was going on and went over to Jack.

'Did you get that from Louis?' she asked. 'I hear Louis say that all the time.'

Jack was about to answer Dolores, but the man wouldn't let up.

'You're a real loser,' he said.

'Losers say "what",' was Jack's response.

'What?' said the man.

'Loser!' cried Jack, laughing again.

The angry man began to laugh hard. Jack let out a sigh of relief and laughed even harder. Then the man became quiet; the look on his face turned severe and threatening. He swung his fist at Jack and knocked Jack to the ground. Paulie caught sight of what was happening and went over to defend Jack. He threw the nasty man a punch right in the jaw. This led to an all-out brawl. The bartender had to call the police to break up the fight, and everyone involved was taken away to jail.

Jack Powell sat in his jail cell, with tears in his eyes. He was cold and confused and he had a humongous headache from the alcohol. He missed his mum and dad and wished he were home in his warm bed.

'Jack Powell,' a police officer called out. 'Your bail was posted, pal. Come on.' And the officer unlocked the cell and led Jack out.

As the officer was giving Jack his possessions back – library card, pocket knife, rabbit's foot, and some sweets – Jack asked where his parents were. But it wasn't his parents that had posted bail. It was Dolores.

'Are you OK?' she asked in a very concerned voice.

'I'm OK.' Jack was embarrassed.

'Louis told me about the new boy in school. He was pretty upset that something had happened to him. Have you heard anything about that?' Dolores asked, trying to make conversation.

'Yeah,' replied Jack. His face was a bright red. He wondered if Dolores knew who he really was.

'Is he going to be OK?' she asked.

'I don't know,' answered Jack after he thought a bit.

Jack and Dolores walked over to her car. Dolores gave Jack a ride home.

'I'm sorry about all this,' said Jack as the car pulled up in front of his house.

'It's O.K. Could I ask you a question?' said Dolores. 'What were you doing there tonight? You seemed lost.'

'It was my first time,' he answered while playing with his house keys.

'I could tell. You should make it your last,' said Dolores, and then she bent over and gave Jack a little kiss on his cheek. 'Now, go on. It's been a long night. I hope I see you at school next time, not at that dive.'

Jack slammed the car door and walked up the path to his home. As he walked through the front door, Karen was there to greet him. She was relieved to see him.

'Jack, where were you?' she asked. 'Your father's out driving around looking for you. You had us worried sick.'

'I'm never going to be a grown-up. And I'm not really a kid. I don't know what I am.' Jack hung his head low, and Karen came over and wrapped her arms around her son. Jack held on to his mother tightly as he stared out the window into the black sky.

14
Shooting Star

THE BIRDS CHIRPED and the smell of freshly baked muffins wafted into Jack's room, but Jack couldn't get himself out of bed. He stayed in bed all morning and part of the afternoon.

Out in the yard, Karen did some gardening. She worked in the garden whenever something was on her mind. As she was planting, Jack's friends arrived at the house. Louis, Edward, George, and John John rode their bikes across the lawn and over to Karen.

'Boys, how are you?' she asked them.

'Hi, Mrs Powell,' they all answered in unison.

'Is Jack home?' asked Louis.

'He's resting,' Karen said in a soft voice.

'Is he coming back to school?' said Louis.

'He needed some time off,' Karen explained. 'The doctor said his heart is still weak. Let me go see if he's up to seeing you.'

Jack wasn't interested in seeing his friends. He didn't want to play. He didn't want to even try to have fun.

As Karen was telling Jack's buddies that he wasn't up to doing anything, Mr Woodruff came by for a visit.

'Hey, Mr Woodruff.' The gang gave him a warm greeting.

'Guys, gimme some skin,' Mr Woodruff said as he held out his hand.

The guys all gave him a friendly slap on the hand before they got on their bikes and rode away.

'Bye, Mr Woodruff. Bye, Mrs Powell,' they called.

When Jack's friends looked like tiny specks in the distance, Karen turned to Mr Woodruff with a concerned look on her face.

'Something's happened,' she told him. 'He won't leave his room. Maybe you could get through to him. Brian and I can't. He's very confused. I think he realized how fragile his life is.'

As Karen spoke to Mr Woodruff, tears welled up

in her eyes. Knowing that her son was in pain was more than Karen could bear.

Mr Woodruff took a handkerchief out of his trouser pocket and held it up to Karen's face. He wiped her tears away and told her that he thought Jack needed to go back to school. But Karen wouldn't listen. She was afraid that if Jack went back the same thing would happen all over again.

Karen and Mr Woodruff approached Jack's bedroom door. They knocked, but there was no answer. Karen opened the door and found Jack sitting with a solemn expression on his face.

'Jack, Mr Woodruff is here,' Karen said softly.

But Jack barely made a gesture to greet his oldest friend and teacher.

Karen let Mr Woodruff in and left the room, closing the door behind her. She knew that if anybody could get through to Jack, Mr Woodruff could.

Mr Woodruff went over to Jack's desk and opened up some textbooks, but Jack refused to sit behind his desk.

'There's no reason for me to learn this stuff if I'm never going to use it,' he said.

'That's not the reason I teach you, Jack,' explained Mr Woodruff in an understanding voice. 'I teach you so you can learn something new and interesting. That's all.'

But Jack said he didn't care about learning any more, and he turned back towards the window.

Mr Woodruff kept trying to lift Jack out of his depression.

'Let's do something else,' he suggested. 'We'll go on the swings outside. Just like we used to.'

'I'm not a kid. Don't treat me like one!' exclaimed Jack.

'You're only ten years old, Jack. I think it's time to play X-Man. Whattaya say?' asked Mr Woodruff.

'No,' replied Jack gloomily.

Then all of a sudden there was a loud noise as Mr Woodruff slammed Jack's maths book closed.

'What are you doing?' asked Jack.

'I'm going home,' said Mr Woodruff as he packed up more of his books and papers.

'You can't quit,' said Jack. He seemed confused by Mr Woodruff's actions.

'Do you know why I like teaching children, Jack?' Mr Woodruff began. 'So I never get too wrapped up in being an adult. So I can remember that there are other things that are important in life. Riding bikes, playing sports, building a tree house.'

Jack looked into Mr Woodruff's eyes and thought about what his teacher was saying.

'And you, my friend, you were my most special pupil. Until recently, you were everything I ever wanted in a pupil,' said Mr Woodruff as he walked over to where Jack was sitting. 'You lived for the moment, like a child should. You were a shooting star among ordinary stars,' he said seriously.

Jack scooted over so there would be room for his teacher to sit. Mr Woodruff sat and looked out of the window with Jack. For a few minutes there was silence, and then Mr Woodruff continued telling Jack his thoughts.

'Did you ever see a shooting star, Jack? Oh, it's wonderful. It passes by quickly, but when it's here, it lights up the whole sky. Most beautiful thing you'd ever see ...' He gazed out of the window and had a look on his face as if he were seeing a shooting star right there and then in the middle of broad daylight. 'It's such a beautiful sight that the other stars actually stop and watch it – so spectacular that people wish upon shooting stars. And they're very rare. You almost never see them, but I did – I saw one.' Mr Woodruff looked directly into Jack's eyes as he told him this.

'I just want to be a regular star,' Jack said sadly, and turned away from his teacher's stare.

'Jack, you're not regular at all,' said Mr Woodruff with a warm smile on his face. 'You're spectacular.'

Mr Woodruff patted Jack on the back and walked out of the room, leaving his pupil alone to think.

In the early evening, the doorbell rang at the Powell house. It was Louis.

'Can Jack come out and play?' he asked. Louis nodded as Karen told him Jack wasn't feeling up to it.

Moments later, there was another ring. This time it was Edward.

'Can Jack come out and play?' he asked.

'No, he can't. I'm sorry,' said Karen.

Then the doorbell rang again and again and

again! Next it was John John, and then George, even Phoebe and Jane. Then more friends from school came by. Jack was very curious about what was going on outside. He looked out of his window. He saw Louis sitting up in the same tree as that time when he and the other guys had believed Jack was a giant. Louis waved wildly at his friend in the window. Jack couldn't help himself. A huge smile appeared on his face, and he waved back to his best friend.

The following day, Jack woke up bright and early, eager to go to school. He changed out of his pyjamas and gave himself a good, clean shave. Jack charged down the steps and into the kitchen. Karen and Brian were taken by surprise to see their son filled with so much energy and happiness.

'I'm going to school,' called Jack as he grabbed an apple. He then ran out of the house and all the way to school.

Everyone in Miss Marquez's class was so happy to see Jack again, including Miss Marquez. Jack handed his teacher a piece of paper. He exchanged high fives with Louis and John John and then took his seat.

Miss Marquez read the piece of paper that Jack handed her. It read: *When I grow up, I want to be Jack*. Miss Marquez nodded approvingly and sent a smile in Jack's direction.

On that day, it was Louis's turn to read his essay. He walked up to the front of the room and began.

'When I grow up, I don't really know what I want to be. But there's one thing I do know – that's *who* I want to be just like when I do grow up.' Louis cleared his throat and continued. 'I want to be just like my best friend when I grow up. He's only ten but he looks much older. He's like the perfect grown-up because on the inside he's still just a kid. It's like he's looking at everything for the first time because he is. And more than anything, he knows how to be a good friend. More than most people who look like adults. So, I may not know what I want to be when I grow up, but I do know who I want to be like. I want to be like the giant, the new kid. I want to be like my best friend, Jack.' Louis glanced over at Jack and smiled.

Jack smiled back at Louis, and as Louis walked past Jack's desk on the way to his own, he placed a small round object on his desk. It was a rubber eyeball! Jack started cracking up, then Louis joined in. The laughing spread, and eventually the entire class was in hysterics.

15
Graduation

A SEA OF purple caps and gowns filled Central High School auditorium. Dolores Durante stood in the middle of a crowd of people pointing her camera at her son.

'Louis, smile,' she called.

Seventeen-year-old Louis stood in his cap and gown waiting to graduate from high school. He was a bit distracted as he looked through the masses of people. He was searching for someone. Then his eyes opened wide as he noticed Jack walking through the crowd. Louis was thrilled that Jack was able to make it to graduation.

Jack was eighteen years old but he looked like an old man of seventy-two. He had snowy grey hair and his face was covered with wrinkles. Jack walked hunched over. Brian and Karen followed their son, and in Karen's hand was the small hand of a little girl – Jack's four-year-old sister!

Jack walked over to his best friend, and the Powells took their seats. Louis giggled as Jack made a funny face at him, and then they got in line with the other graduates who were waiting to accept their diplomas.

The principal of the high school introduced the guest speaker. It was Mr Woodruff, a Central High graduate. Mr Woodruff addressed the graduating class, and when he was done, he called upon the valedictorian to speak.

Jack Powell walked up to the microphone and cleared his throat. He put on a pair of reading glasses and took out a bunch of note cards.

'Go get 'em, Jack,' a voice called out from the crowd.

Jack smiled and began to speak.

'I don't have much time these days, so I'll just keep it short,' he began. 'As these final days wear down, we think of times forgotten, and we pray for new beginnings. And some of us worry about our future. But I say, let us not worry, because in the end none of us has very long on this earth. Life is fleeting. And if you're ever distressed, cast your eyes to the summer sky, when the stars are strung across the velvety night, and when a shooting star streaks through the blackness turning night into day, make a wish and think of me. Make your lives spectacular. I know I did.'

THE DEMON HEADMASTER STRIKES AGAIN
Gillian Cross

The villainous genius is back at his desk!

He's back, and he's very, very dangerous.

Dinah's father is headhunted for a new job at the Biodiversity Research Centre – and who should be the Director, but the Demon Headmaster . . .

This time his lust for power sees him meddling with evolution itself. The consequences of his evil schemes will be deadly if the SPLAT gang doesn't act – and fast.

JAMES AND THE GIANT PEACH
Roald Dahl

Now an amazing Disney film!

Something is about to happen, James told himself. Something peculiar is about to happen at any moment.

James has lived with his two beastly aunts ever since the day his parents were eaten up outside London Zoo by an angry escaped rhinoceros. Aunt Sponge and Aunt Spiker are really horrible people. They make poor James's life a misery.

Then something very peculiar happens – something magical that is to completely change James's wretched existence and take him on the most amazing and unbelievable journey!

A classic story perfectly illustrated by Quentin Blake.

MATILDA
Roald Dahl

Now a wonderful film

There began to creep over Matilda a most extraordinary and peculiar feeling . . . a kind of electricity . . .

Matilda is an exceptional girl, but her parents think she is just a nuisance. When one day she is attacked by her odious headmistress, Miss Trunchbull, Matilda discovers she has a remarkable power with which to avenge herself!

The captivating story of an unforgettable girl, perfectly complemented with illustrations by Quentin Blake.

MATT'S MILLION
Andrew Norriss

Now a brilliant TV series

Dear Matthew, I have great pleasure in enclosing a cheque, made out to your name, for the sum of £1,227,309.87.

Matt Collins is eleven years old, and a millionaire! Suddenly he has the money to buy anything he wants – a mansion or even a Rolls-Royce. But being rich is more difficult than he thought.

THE ADVENTURES OF PINOCCHIO™
Carlo Collodi

A novelization by J. J. Gardner

Based on the screenplay by Sherry Mills and Steve Barron and Tom Benedek and Barry Berman

"You're a puppet, Pinocchio – you're not a real boy."

Pinocchio is a special puppet. He can walk and talk, and his nose grows when he tells a lie! However, more than anything in the world, he wants to be a real boy.

Before Pinocchio's wish can come true he must prove he has a heart. He has to learn to tell the truth and care enough to cry real tears. But, with the help of a talking cricket, Pinocchio learns that miracles can happen.

THE SHEEP-PIG/ACE
Dick King-Smith

**Meet BABE
The Sheep-Pig
and ACE,
his great-grandson**

Two very special pigs.

Babe – polite, well-mannered and very good at looking after sheep.

Ace – Babe's great-grandson, who likes nothing better than watching television.

WIND IN THE WILLOWS
NOVELISATION
Adapted by Nancy Krulik

From the screenplay by Terry Jones

Based on the novel by Kenneth Grahame

The fastest Toad on the road!

Life along the river bank is quiet and relaxing.
That is, until poor Mole has his home destroyed
and Toad discovers motor cars.

What follows is a thrilling adventure, as Ratty,
Mole and Badger try to save Toad from himself
and Toad Hall from destruction.

Based on the classic story by Kenneth Grahame
and the film starring Terry Jones.

LITTLE WOMEN
Louisa May Alcott
Adapted by Robin Waterfield

Times are hard for the March girls

Growing up is often a difficult business. Jo,
Meg, Amy and Beth have to cope with their
family's lack of money and also miss their
father who is away at war. They try to
overcome these problems by doing new and
exciting things, determined that when their
father returns, they will really
be 'Little Women'.

This classic story of four American girls and
their adventures has been retold many times as
a film and on television: this version is a
faithful adaptation of the original book.

MADAME DOUBTFIRE
Anne Fine

'A vast apparition towered over her on the doorstep. It wore a loose salmon pink coat ... and tucked under its arm was an enormous imitation crocodile skin handbag ... "I'm Madame Doubtfire, dear."'

Lydia, Christopher and Natalie Hilliar are used to domestic turmoil and have been torn between their warring parents ever since the divorce. But all that changes when their mother takes on a most unusual cleaning lady.

Despite her extraordinary appearance, Madame Doubtfire turns out to be a talented and efficient housekeeper and, for a short time at least, the arrangement is a resounding success. But, as the Hilliard children soon discover, there's more to Madame Doubtfire than domestic talents . . .

READ MORE IN PUFFIN

For children of all ages, Puffin represents quality and variety – the very best in publishing today around the world.

For complete information about books available from Puffin – and Penguin – and how to order them, contact us at the appropriate address below. Please note that for copyright reasons the selection of books varies from country to country.

On the world wide web: www.penguin.co.uk

In the United Kingdom: Please write to *Dept. EP, Penguin Books Ltd, Bath Road, Harmondsworth, West Drayton, Middlesex UB7 ODA*

In the United States: Please write to *Consumer Sales, Penguin USA, P.O. Box 999, Dept. 17109, Bergenfield, New Jersey 07621-0120*. VISA and MasterCard holders call 1-800-253-6476 to order Penguin titles

In Canada: Please write to *Penguin Books Canada Ltd, 10 Alcorn Avenue, Suite 300, Toronto, Ontario M4V 3B2*

In Australia: Please write to *Penguin Books Australia Ltd, P.O. Box 257, Ringwood, Victoria 3134*

In New Zealand: Please write to *Penguin Books (NZ) Ltd, Private Bag 102902, North Shore Mail Centre, Auckland 10*

In India: Please write to *Penguin Books India Pvt Ltd, 706 Eros Apartments, 56 Nehru Place, New Delhi 110 019*

In the Netherlands: Please write to *Penguin Books Netherlands bv, Postbus 3507, NL-1001 AH Amsterdam*

In Germany: Please write to *Penguin Books Deutschland GmbH, Metzlerstrasse 26, 60594 Frankfurt am Main*

In Spain: Please write to *Penguin Books S. A., Bravo Murillo 19, 1° B, 28015 Madrid*

In Italy: Please write to *Penguin Italia s.r.l., Via Felice Casati 20, I–20124 Milano*

In France: Please write to *Penguin France S. A., 17 rue Lejeune, F–31000 Toulouse*

In Japan: Please write to *Penguin Books Japan, Ishikiribashi Building, 2-5-4, Suido, Bunkyo-ku, Tokyo 112*

In South Africa: Please write to *Longman Penguin Southern Africa (Pty) Ltd, Private Bag X08, Bertsham 2013*